It's Just a Bunnypalooza

written by Brenda Faatz & Peter Trimarco
illustrated by Peter Trimarco

Printed in the USA

For Chandler, Tad and Jon.

Copyright ©2019 by Peter Trimarco and Brenda Faatz.
All rights reserved. Published by Notable Kids Publishing, LLC.
No part of this publication may be reproduced in any form without written permission of the copyright owner or publisher.
For information write to Notable Kids Publishing, Box 2047, Parker, Colorado 80134

ISBN-13: 978-0-9970851-7-4
[Juvenile Fiction – ages 3-8]

Library of Congress Control Number: 2018914864
Faatz, Brenda & Trimarco, Peter
It's Just a Bunnypalooza / written by Brenda Faatz / Peter Trimarco and illustrated by Peter Trimarco – 1st ed.
Summary: It's Just a Bunnypalooza for Lizzy, the ever rambunctious and creative protagonist. When Lizzy shares how she's learning dance moves from her bunny friends, she is embarrassed as children giggle at her over-active imagination. She then becomes an avid "non-believer" until the neighborhood bunnies decide to organize an intervention!

Printed in the USA by Worzalla, Stevens Point Wisconsin
Typography: Museo 300, Cooper, American Typewriter, Comic Sans
The illustrations were done with pen & ink on bristol board, with backgrounds painted in acrylic on canvas.
Spot colors and additional finish work created in photoshop. Etcha-sketch was not used in any form, nor were any bunnies harmed in the creation of this book of fiction.
Lizzy Character ©2015 - 2019 Faatz & Trimarco

It's just...

...about time.

It's just...

...tick **tock torture!**

Lizzy flew out the door—not a moment to lose, and ran home to her friends to announce the BIG NEWS!

In Lizzy's backyard, they all scurried together.
She spoke to her friends of fur, fleece and feather.

"In the spring of each year at the school where I go
comes the biggest event, the SPRING JAMBOREE SHOW!
All the kids can perform and I want to play too,
but I need your help finding a talent to do."

"Yes, of course!" Lizzy said,
"I will chirp like a bird."
So she puckered and puffed...
but just SPLIT-SPLAT was heard.

It's just so...
pffffPPPptttth!

"Or...like an elk I could bugle, or grunt like a moose."
But her big brassy BLURT shook the moose antlers loose.

snork!

"To hoot like an owl, that's a thing I can do."
But exciting, it's NOT –
just one word, simply Whooooooooooooo

"Or...I could hum like a hummingbird, zipping about.
But this waving my arms is just wearing me out!"

It's just so...
flipflappy-fast!

"I could twirl with the squirrels
like a flying trapeze.
But swinging through trees
is NOT coming with ease."

o....Dizzzee-Queeeeeeeeeeeeeeeeeezzzy!

Then she noticed
some bunnies
with feet in the air.
"Yes, of course!" Lizzy said.
"Bunnies dance – and with flair!
They leap and they hop
and they turn
and they stomp.
They can teach me!"

It's
just
a
jig
fabulo
romp!

It's just so...

...toe tappin'

...jump jivin'

...free stylin'

...beboppin'

...bunnybombastic!

Kids gathered together at school the next day
sharing plans for the talents that they would display.
"I'll be SINGING!" "I'm JUGGLING!" "I'm PLAYING PIANO!"
"With Mozart!" "With fruit!" "With my sky-high soprano!"

Lizzy waited her turn and then chimed in with glee,
"I'll be DANCING!
The bunnies! They're all teaching me!"
As she shared how the cottontails taught her to wiggle,
she noticed her friends were beginning to giggle.

Lizzy's tummy felt twisty and to her surprise
her happy was gone as tears welled in her eyes.
She stood by herself feeling lost and confused.
"Are they laughing at me?"
Lizzy's heart - it felt bruised.

"I'm so silly to think bunnies dance, teach and play.
Imagining doesn't just make it that way.
Enough of this crazy! It's time to be grown.
No more listening to critters.
I'll go it alone!"

But...

Lizzy's 'go alone plan'
would not last very long,
as the underground movement
of bunnies was strong.

They could not let Lizzy
give up on her gifts.
To help her, the bunnies
would need to be swift.

Their mission was clear, they had magic to weave.

For Lizzy to see,
she would need to believe.

So they sprang to a jig, hoping Lizzy would glance,
doing bunny hop, hora, and milk bottle dance.

It's just so.... Jigga-Wiggalous.

Then the bunnies jumped into a full-on ballet.
They twisted and turned with a leap and a sway.

It's just a.... Ballet-hoo!

But Lizzy did not see the tap or soft shoe
or tango, fandango, hip hop boogaloo.

And she would not look when they danced the mazurka,
not even when bunnies went wildly BAZURKA.

It's just a.... POLKA-LOCA FRENZY!

When the day finally came for the Spring Jamboree,
Lizzy headed for school, but she STILL did not see.
So to help her remember her strength deep within
a new plan was formed and about to begin.

Oh...

Then Lizzy, who could not and would not believe,
STOPPED when a bunny hopped onto her sleeve.
She looked to her heart and was able to see.
"I can dance to my rhythm and choose to be me!"

Lizzy trusted and followed her feelings inside, with her dancing, imagining heart as her guide.

She heard laughter and giggles from friends all around,
and this time the laughter was such a sweet sound.

Bunny Dance Glossary

Ballet - Origin: Italian Renaissance Courts. Ballet first began over 600 years ago and was performed at parties for Bunny Royalty.

Beboppin' - Origin: New Orleans, USA. This quick and fancy foot work (or in this case, "paw" work) is danced to crazy fast jazz music.

Bharatanatyam - Origin: India. This 1800 year-old dance is also called "The Fire Dance," because the movements look like a dancing flame.

Boogaloo - Origin: New York City, USA. Boogaloo is a form of hip hop dance where the dancers circle their hips and legs, adding steps, kicks, and upper body moves to show their own style. Lizzy LOVES this dance, but very few bunnies are bold enough to boogaloo.

Bottle Dance - Origin: USA and Paraguay. The famous "bottle dance" from the Broadway musical *Fiddler on the Roof* was created especially for that show. There is also a traditional "bottle dance" performed by women in Paraguay. The bunny bottle dance in this story uses real milk bottles!

Breakdancing - Origin: The Bronx, NY, USA. Breakdancing, also known as 'breaking,' is the oldest form of hip hop dance. The people who perform this dance are known as *breakers*, or *b-boys* and *b-girls*.

Bunny Hop - Origin: This dance was made up at a high school in San Francisco, CA, USA, to go with a song of the same name. There is also a Finnish folk dance called *Letkis* using almost exactly the same moves. We think they all learned this dance from their rabbit friends, just like Lizzy did.

Bunnypalooza - Origin: Lizzy's World! The authors of this book made up this word. What do you think it means?

Disco Dancing - Origin: New York City, USA. Many popular disco moves were inspired by Latin dances like the the samba, cha cha, and tango. This dance was made popular by the movie *Saturday Night Fever (Bunny Edition)!*

Fandango - Origin: Spain. The word *fandango* is also sometimes used to mean "a quarrel," or a "a big fuss," so if you look out your window and see some bunnies in a tussle, they just may be doing a fandango!

Free Stylin' - Origin: On street corners of Los Angeles and New York City, USA. This dance is about "making it up as you go along" and can refer to anything, not just dancing. We recommend you do at least one *free stylin'* thing every day!

Hip Hop - Origin: New York City, and later in California, USA. Hip hop dancing originally started with young people on street corners in the Bronx, New York, as a positive way to express themselves. There are those among the underground bunny brigade who strongly feel that *they* originated this dance style.

Hora - Origin: Balkans in Southeast Europe. The hora is a circle dance usually enjoyed at celebrations by varied cultures in many countries. Bunnies in this story are showing you what sometimes happens in the center of the circle… using a sheet to bounce each other in the air! Do you know what these bunnies are wearing on their heads?

Jig - Origin: Scotland and Northern England and later in Ireland. A jig is a lively, festive dance with a lot of hopping, kicking, and foot shuffling…. A perfect dance for bunnies!

Jump-jivin' - Origin: USA in the 1950s. This is a swing dance where people (and bunnies) kick up their heels, spin, and fling each other into the air.

Mazurka - Origin: Poland. The music that goes with this folk dance is also called a mazurka. Turn to the mazurka page in this book and decide if the word that rhymes with mazurka is a REAL word or a made up word.

Polka - Origin: Eastern Bohemia (now part of the Czech Republic). It is believed the polka was invented by a peasant girl, just for fun. Our polka bunny is playing an accordion because these instruments are an important part of polka music. There is also a dance called the polka-mazurka!

Rumba - Origin: With roots in Africa and Spain, this dance was made popular in Cuba. The word "rumba" comes from the verb "rumbear" which means going to parties, dancing, and having a good time - all things that bunnies LOVE to do!

Soft Shoe - Origin: USA. Soft shoe dancing is the quiet version of tap dancing. It is done without the taps (see "Tap Dance" below).

Tango - Origin: From Argentina and Uruguay. Tango dance is one of the most popular dances in the entire world and enjoyed by humans and bunnies alike.

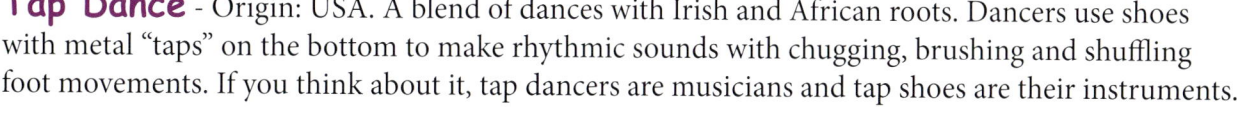
Tap Dance - Origin: USA. A blend of dances with Irish and African roots. Dancers use shoes with metal "taps" on the bottom to make rhythmic sounds with chugging, brushing and shuffling foot movements. If you think about it, tap dancers are musicians and tap shoes are their instruments.

Toe Tappin' - Origin: Everywhere in the world. This happens when any kind of music you're listening to makes you tap your paws uncontrollably.

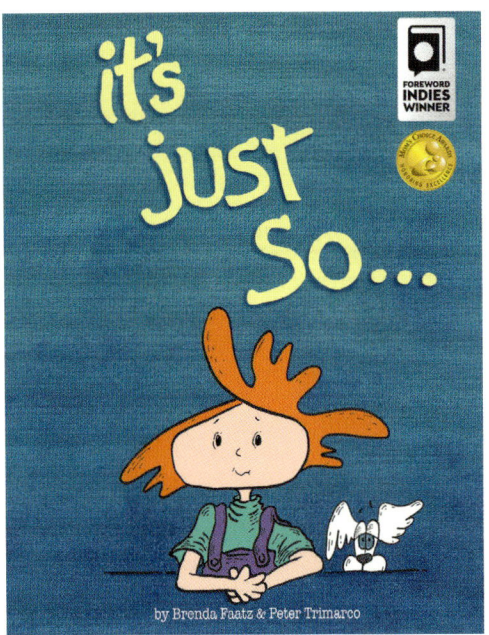

It's just so…

by Brenda Faatz & Peter Trimarco
ISBN-13: 9780997085105
Library of Congress: 2015919850
©2016 / Published April 16, 2016

It's Lizzy's first day in a brand new school! At first things feel "just so" scary and "just so" hard, but in the end, they're "just so"…. not what she thought they would be!

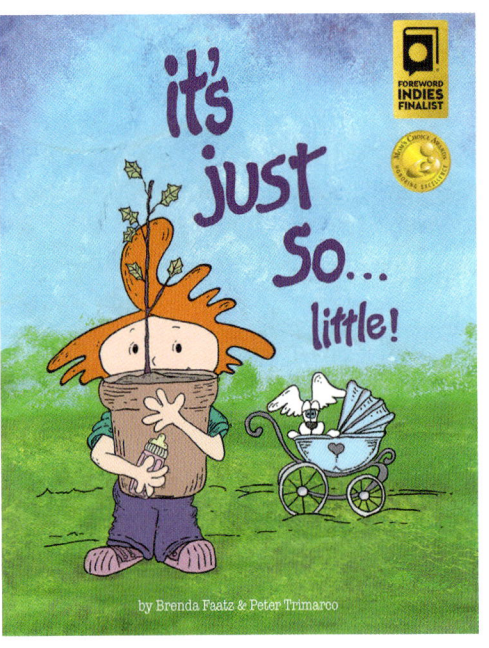

It's just so…little!

by Brenda Faatz & Peter Trimarco
ISBN-13: 9780997085129
Library of Congress: 2016919569
©2017 / Published May 23, 2017

Lizzy faces challenges of growth and change as she prepares to become a big sister. In the meantime, she and her faithful puppy nurture a frail sapling tree over the course of a year.

www.itsjustso.net / www.lizzysworld.net / notablekidspublishing.com / facebook/itsjustsobooks

Through the magic of Augmented Reality, children can bring Lizzy to life in their own homes!
Download "Lizzy's World" Augmented Reality reading & game app —
Created in partnership with Playing Forward — in the Apple iOS or Google Play app stores.